SANDRA DIECKMANN
WAITING for WOLF

Hodder
Children's
Books

Fox played with Wolf by the big blue lake.
The sun shone down on the two friends.

They talked and laughed for hours, and afterwards

they swam in the warm water until they were tired.

Days always seemed bright when Fox was with Wolf.

"Life really is beautiful," said Wolf.
"Oh, yes," said Fox. "It always is when we are together!"

"Promise me," said Wolf, "you'll always remember
this perfect day." Fox nodded happily.

That evening, the two friends watched the stars come out
one by one. Wolf put his big, grey paw on Fox's shoulder
and said quietly, "Tomorrow I will be starlight."

Fox didn't understand.

For now, it was just good to be together
and Wolf said nothing more.

The next day, Fox went to look for Wolf.
She was excited to see him all shiny and sparkling like a star.

She went to his den.
It was cold and empty.

She searched all day,

but Wolf was nowhere to be found.

No one had seen him.

Fox went down to their favourite spot by the lake.

She didn't know what to do, so she waited for Wolf.

A single star shone out brighter than all the others, which made her wonder.

"He said he was going to be starlight.

So maybe he's up there in the sky!"

Fox set off into the mountains,
towards the brightest star
in the night sky.

She climbed, and climbed, until she reached the highest peak.

She called into the starry sky, "WOOOLF!"
There was no answer. So she yelled louder into the crushing silence . . .

"WHERE ARE YOU?"

she cried.

She reached up to the stars

and pulled the shining star blanket

down from the sky.

Everything

went

dark.

She sat there for a long time, wrapped
in the velvety star blanket.

"Wolf ...
are you there?"
she whispered.

There was no answer.

Fox did not call for Wolf again.
In her heart, she knew that Wolf
was never coming back.

Tears rolled down her cheeks and trickled over the mountainside to the lake. Suddenly, the stars in the velvety blanket shimmered and flickered

Fox could just make out her little red paw in the darkness.

It was **bright**
and **red**
and **alive!**

"Life really is beautiful," whispered Fox,
remembering Wolf's words on that last perfect day together.

Suddenly, all the things they had done together
came flooding back in bright colours.

Fox knew she wasn't going to stay in the darkness any longer.

She wanted to swim in the blue lake and run along the yellow sand.

Fox put the star blanket gently back where it belonged.

The moon shone down peacefully over the lake and the stars danced in the sky

At last, Fox understood what Wolf had said.

He was gone, but all the wonderful things they had shared together would be with her **always**.

Fox smiled as she
remembered her friend Wolf.